The Not Very Merry Pout-Pout Fish

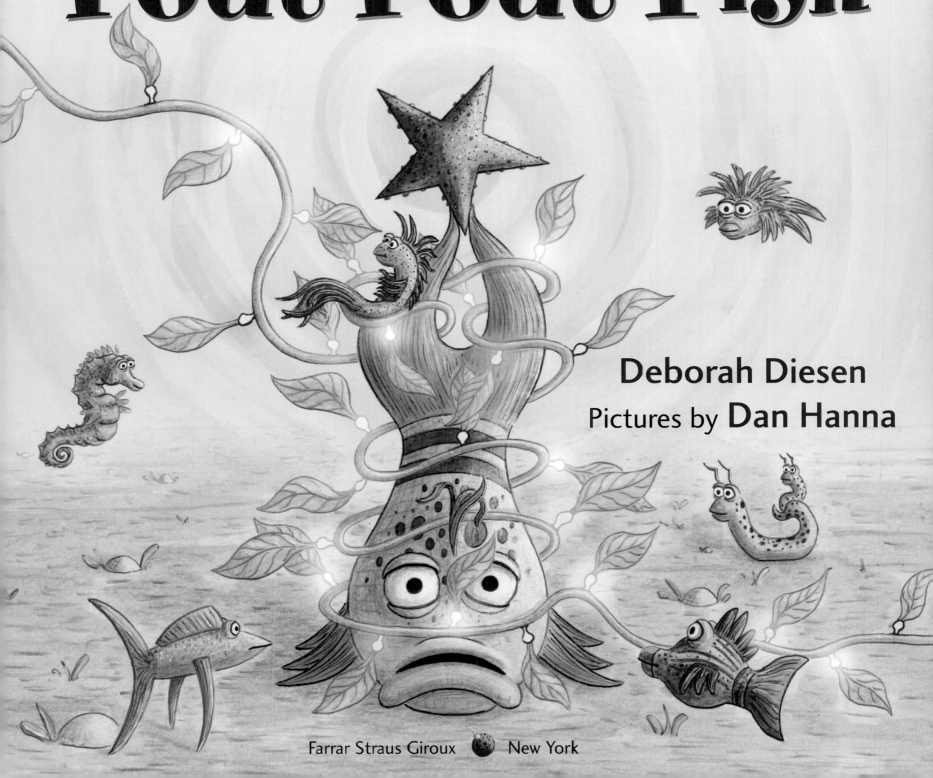

Deborah Diesen

Pictures by Dan Hanna

Farrar Straus Giroux • New York

For Joan and for Dave.
Thank you for the gift of friendship —D.D.

To Janine O'Malley, editor extraordinaire,
for giving me the wonderful gift of The Pout-Pout Fish *—D.H.*

Farrar Straus Giroux Books for Young Readers
175 Fifth Avenue, New York 10010

Text copyright © 2015 by Deborah Diesen
Pictures copyright © 2015 by Dan Hanna
All rights reserved
Color separations by Embassy Graphics
Printed in China by RR Donnelley Asia Printing Solutions Ltd.,
Dongguan City, Guangdong Province
Designed by Roberta Pressel
First edition, 2015
10 9 8 7 6 5 4 3 2

mackids.com

Library of Congress Cataloging-in-Publication Data
Diesen, Deborah.
    The not very merry pout-pout fish : a pout-pout fish adventure /
Deborah Diesen ; pictures by Dan Hanna. — First edition.
        pages cm.
    Summary: "Mr. Fish is having a hard time finding the right presents for his friends, until
he learns that the best gifts come from the heart" —Provided by publisher.
    ISBN 978-0-374-35549-4 (hardcover)
    [1. Stories in rhyme.   2. Gifts—Fiction.   3. Fishes—Fiction.   4. Marine animals—Fiction.
5. Christmas—Fiction.]   I. Hanna, Dan, illustrator.   II. Title.

PZ8.3.D565Not 2015
[E]—dc23   2014032836

Farrar Straus Giroux Books for Young Readers may be purchased for business or promotional use.
For information on bulk purchases please contact Macmillan Corporate and Premium Sales Department
at (800) 221-7945 x5442 or by email at specialmarkets@macmillan.com.

In a festive ocean corner,
Fish were decking out the reef,
Hanging tinsel, bows, and lights
In a holiday motif.

Voices laughed! Voices sang!
What a merry time of year!
Yet a certain gloomy fish
Wasn't feeling any cheer.

Mr. Fish, with his list,
Wore a yuletide pout:
"I need presents for my friends,
But my time is running out!

"For a gift should be *big*,
And a gift should be *bright*.
And a gift should be *perfect*—
Guaranteed to bring delight.

"And a gift should have *meaning*
Plus a bit of bling-*zing*,
So I'll shop till I drop
For each just-right thing!"

At the first store he reached,
Mr. Fish's eyes grew wide.
The shelves were full of baubles.
How could *any* fish decide!

Shiny trinkets! Handy gadgets!
Choices more and more galore!
And yet nothing seemed quite right.
"Guess I'll try the shop next door.

"For a gift should be *big*,
And a gift should be *bright*.
And a gift should be *perfect*—
Guaranteed to bring delight.

"And a gift should have *meaning*
Plus a bit of bling-*zing,*
So I'll shop till I drop
For each just-right thing!"

In a tizzy-busy crowd,
Shoppers everywhere beside him,
Mr. Fish spied a banner
For the season's hottest item.

GIANT HOLIDAY FUN BALLS!

While Supplies Last

MAW MALL

OPEN

He hustle-bustled over—
But they'd just sold out!
Mr. Fish's hopes wobbled
In a bout of pout-doubt.

"For a gift should be *big*,
And a gift should be *bright*.
And a gift should be *perfect*—
Guaranteed to bring delight.

"And a gift should have *meaning*
Plus a bit of bling-*zing*,
So I'll shop till I drop
For each just-right thing!"

He reached the final store,
And was very first in line!
But his shopping plans were dashed . . .
"We're closed" said the sign!

There were no stores left!
There was no place to go!
Mr. Fish had *nothing*—
Not a single gift to show!

"Oh, a gift should be *big*,
And a gift should be *bright*.
And a gift should be *perfect*—
Guaranteed to bring delight.

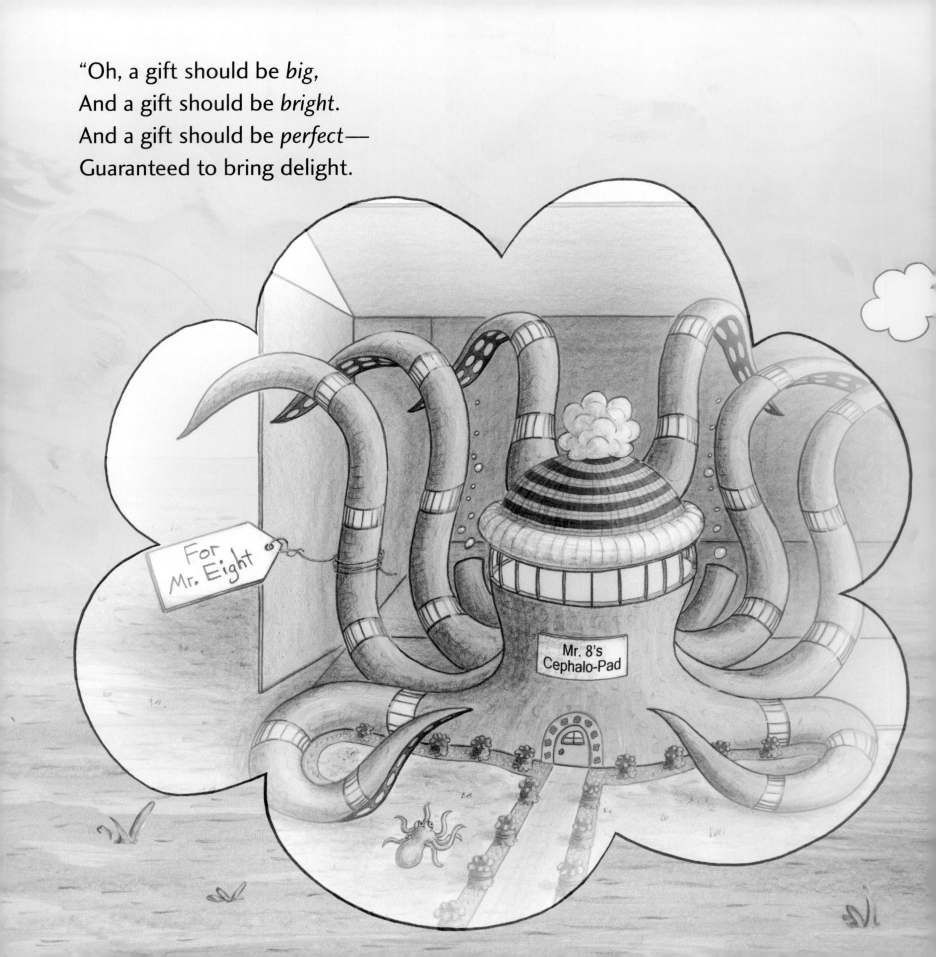

"And a gift should have *meaning*
Plus a bit of bling-*zing*,
But I've shopped till I've plopped
And I don't have a thing!"

Mr. Fish's face sank
In a crestfallen frown.
"I'll have to miss the party.
I've let *all* my friends down!"

Then a gentle voice jingled:
"Mr. Fish, not true!
All you *really* need to bring
Is the one and only YOU!

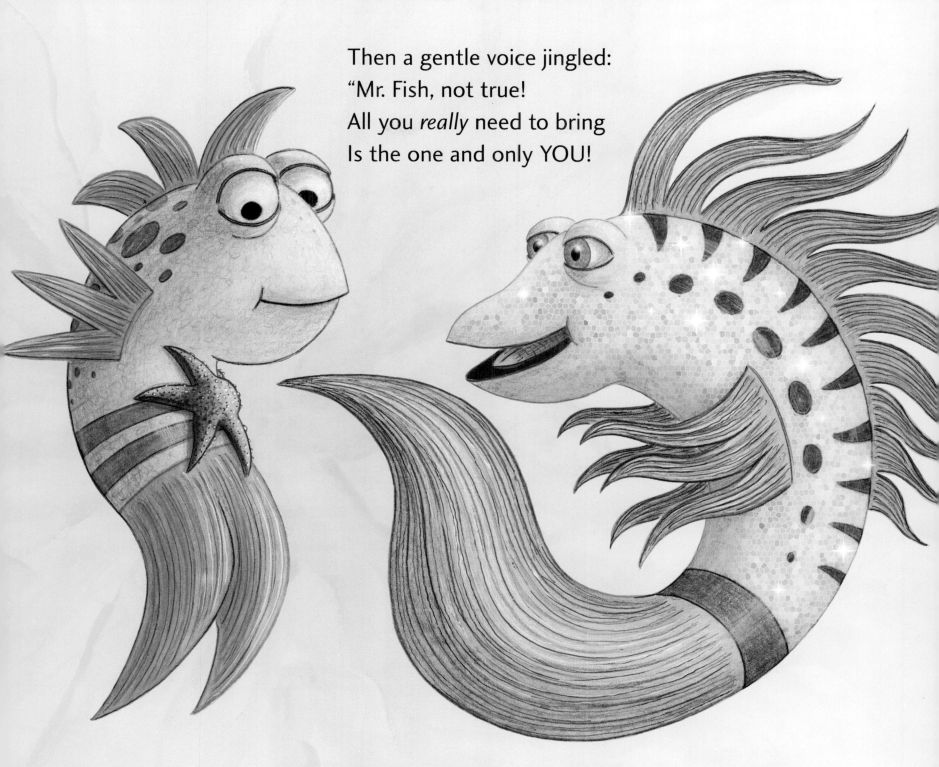

"If you want to give some presents
It is not too late to start,
For the best gifts of all
Come straight from the heart."

With the help of Miss Shimmer,
Sharing laughter, fun, and grins,

Mr. Fish *made* gifts
With his very own fins!

Later at the party,
Mr. Fish passed them out,
And he felt very merry:
"This is what today's about!"

For his gifts were *big*,
And his gifts were *bright*.
And his gifts were *perfect*—
And they all brought delight!

For
Mrs. Squid

And his gifts had *meaning*
Plus a bit of bling-*zing*,

And his each and every friend loved
Their just-right thing.

For Mr. Eight

For Ms. Clam

All were happy. All were laughing.
All were talking. All were singing.

All were sharing in the season
And the goodwill it was bringing.

Mr. Fish joined his friends
And he felt his heart lift:
They had peace, joy, and love—